Parable of the FOXES

DEJI ADEYEYE, ESQ.

NATIONAL LIBRARY OF NIGERIA CATALOGU-ING-IN-PUBLICATION DATA

Parable of the foxes
ADEYEYE, Deji 1981-
1. Nigerian prose literature (English)
2. Self-actualization (Psychology)
I. Title

PR9387.9.A233 P221	2024	829.8
ISBN: 978-978-62019-4-8	(pbk)	AACR2

Parable of the Foxes

ISBN: 978-978-62019-4-8

Published and printed by:

Pen-Impact Writing and Publishing Enterprise
16 Adedoyin Rhodes-Vivour Close, Asokoro,
Abuja, FCT, Nigeria
Website: www.pen-impact.com
Email: info@pen-impact.com
Tel: +234 701 990 4999

CHAPTER ONE

A voice rapped audibly behind the tent's door, "Lazy bones, it's time to wake up!" Amah's dream was interrupted. It was his brother, Benju, who was calling to him. Amah slowly turned around on the all-wooden bed he slept on, bewildered and his mind full of dreams.

"It must be 4 a.m. now, "Amah grumbled. His voice was thick with sleep.

"What did you say?" Benju burst out laughing from behind the door. "It's ten o'clock now!"

"Impossible! Wait." Amah stumbled out of his thin, two-legged bed that had its other two legs buried into the wooden pillar of the tent. He reached for an old cloth to wear before putting his hand on the door to open it and meet his brother. He saw Benju standing and laughing at him wildly.

"Sleeping all morning!" Benju teased. "I told you not to plough too much yesterday. But you always insisted you must do some more. Small boys like you shouldn't do that."

Amah looked over to Benju in the dirty clothes he wore, almost as black as his skin. That suggested to him that it was time to venture deep into the forest to pick nuts and berries. The fruits were always abundant for people to eat in the forest. Only a few dwellers of the forest had discovered where the fruits were. Those who knew where to find the fruits lived on them. Others lived on animals, which were trapped every night to make the next day's meal.

However difficult living in this forest was, it was far better than living in the villages where the dwellers of this forest had come from. The number of people living in the forest was very few at first. But as war became more frequent in the villages nearer to the forest, the people increased in the forest. They were mostly men in their twenties and thirties. They were the few ones strong enough to escape the infernos that engulfed their villages. The aged, the women and the children had perished in blazes.

For the first time, Amah's mind woke up completely. "It must be time to go and pick fruits," he said.

Benju nodded. "Aren't you going today?"

Immediately, Amah turned back and looked at his bed, where he had slept, dreaming. He looked back at Benju, who was still teasing him with laughter.

"Do you want to go back to sleep?" Benju asked. "I don't mind. I'll go out alone to pick the fruits."

Amah could not tell his brother to go without him, but he really wanted to be alone. They had grown so close that it was hard for them to stay apart. Now, the forest had brought them closer since they were the only two in their family who had survived the war.

They were the last two of eight children in their family. Their six older brothers died in a single war between their village, Orile and its neighbour, Abiri. What caused the war was a large piece of land bigger than either of the two villages, which stretched by their boundary. On this piece of land grew numerous palm trees that had served as food for animals long before they settled there.

It was the control of this virgin land that pushed the young men of Orile and Abiri to war. Their elders urged them on. All men in their teens and prime from both villages were drafted into the war. It lasted four years. At first, Abiri took the upper hand, slaughtering Orile men in great numbers. Then, the six brothers fell in one swoop. The news reached home, crippling their father, Josi and making their pregnant mother sick. The old men in Orile immediately sued for peace to save their young men. But Abiri refused the peace offer and decided to wipe out its enemy and possess all the fortunes alone. It had everything to conquer its foes.

At the battlefront, the few men left in Orile fought on, and the table turned. Then, it was Abiri's turn to sue for peace. But it was too late. Orile fought until it had totally destroyed its enemies, going deep into Abiri and setting the houses and farms ablaze. The war heroes returned singing, and the whole village met them like the real war heroes that they were with drumming and dancing. The wailing that had earlier filled the village with the news of fallen valiant young men changed to jubilation of war victory.

Crippled Josi heard the jubilation where he sat. The sad news of his sons' death flooded his mind once more, and he shed tears in silence. His sick wife, carrying her ninth child in her belly, staggered out to the front door of their hut. She leaned on the pillar of the hut and peered into the distant horizon, looking for nothing in particular. She wished her sons, or just one of them, could be among the returning war heroes. She knew that was a vain wish. She would never see them again. She shook her head in pity. She loved to live to care for her crippled husband, two remaining sons and unborn child. Her health made her doubt that possibility. Everything in her body told her that she would die soon - sooner than she wished.

As the sun dipped below the horizon, she made it a point to spend quality time with her sons, offering them words of encouragement and reassurance. With a gentle smile and a warm embrace, she promised them that she would defy mortality and live long enough to witness their transformation into becoming outstanding individuals, respected and admired by their community. She envisioned their future success and the pride it would bring her, and this thought filled her heart with joy and her spirit with determination.

Josi loved to die before his wife and leave her with all his belongings to care for their surviving children. He knew he was not old enough to die. Not as old as his father, who lived to be one hundred years old, or his grandfather, who lived to be ninety. He was just fifty. But he had seen more misery than they had both seen. He often said this to his children before the unforgettable carnage took away all six of them.

Now, Josi lived with the fear that he might lose his wife. Two weeks after the triumphant return of the war heroes, Josi began to mourn his wife. She had fallen into labour but was too weak to be delivered of the child. She pushed and pushed, but the child refused to come out of her. At last, the child's head was coming out, but she could push no more. The baby was pulled out by her neighbours. Mother and child were silent.

Josi buried his wife and the stillborn child near his sons' graves. He continued raising his surviving sons. That was over ten years ago when Amah was a little boy of eight and Benju twelve. Both boys had a clear memory of that. But it was not their worst memory yet.

CHAPTER TWO

When he fully realised what time of the morning it was, Amah said disappointingly, "I can't believe I slept till now."

"I was surprised too," replied Benju. "But that's bound to happen if one's too greedy with work, wanting to do everything at once..."

"I don't think that's the reason." Amah disagreed. "I'd worked for the whole day before, like I did yesterday, without oversleeping the following morning."

"If you don't believe me, there's no trouble," Benju said. "I know that I'm correct. I hope you'll listen for once and stop overworking yourself. We don't need to labour too much in this forest. There's already enough for us to eat."

"But we can't depend solely on what's in the forest. We need to plough and sow more seeds for the future. One day, there will be more people in the forest, and what the forest has now will not be enough for them. That's what our father taught us: to prepare well for the future. Even if there's abundance now, we must still sow for the future." Amah said.

"And you think father was right?" Asked Benju.

"Yes, he was," Amah replied. "He spent his whole life labouring for our future. I could recollect how he planted and brought in large quantities of yams and maize that he lay in great piles in barns for us and the big orchards he planted."

"Where's the future our father laboured for now?" asked Benju.

"The future's here with us," said Amah sharply. "We are the future!"

"No," Benju said. "The future he laboured for has gone with him. It has gone in that fire."

"Not really," disagrees Amah. "The fire only consumed our father's house and farms and barns but not his dreams. He had a dream that one day, the wars would stop. Valiant young men would not lose their lives anymore. We can live in peace and not die."

"I wish we could," said Benju, shaking his head. "But I fear we can't. This peaceful forest will one day go in smoke like our village did."

Two years after the victorious war against Abiri, Orile suffered a self-inflicted demise, unlike its defeated enemy. The downfall of Orile was not caused by external forces but by internal strife. The conflict arose from a dispute over control and distribution of the newfound wealth acquired from the conquered palm trees that had brought immense fortune to Orile. The spoils of war, meant to be a blessing, became a curse as the people of Orile fought among themselves, ultimately leading to their own downfall. The High Chief, in a gesture of respect, had relinquished the decision-making power to the council of elders. However, the young men who had bravely fought in the war and returned victorious began to vociferously assert their claim to have a say in the decision. They argued that having risked their lives to secure the community's triumph; they should have a significant role in determining the course of action. This sudden intervention by the young warriors effectively challenged the authority of the elders and the High Chief's initial decision.

The young men were forbidden to speak with their representatives and ordered to leave the presence of the elders. Then they raised their arms. They had all their lives laboured for the elders and leaders on their farms for the owners and their children to enjoy. They had thought that the war spoils would liberate them and make them the leaders. That had inspired them to risk their lives and go to war. They were not willing to part with what they thought was rightly theirs. As the elders and leaders took their stand to control the wealth of the land, the young men took their stand to fight.

Week after week, the vast farms belonging to the elders, where the young men had toiled to plough and cultivate the land, were set ablaze in a series of deliberate acts of arson, aimed at coercing the elders to surrender to the young men's demands. But the wealth was too much to give to young men who would squander it all. The chiefs and elders knew they were no longer safe. The battle line had been drawn.

Josi had lived with one sense of achievement: that he had lost his sons to secure a life-long fortune for his village. Now, the village had just lost peace to keep its fortune, and this baffled him.

Able-bodied men and women fled from Orile as they had from Abiri and ran across the river into the deep jungle. From there, as they looked back, they saw thick smoke billowing high into the sky, a stark reminder of the destruction they had left behind. The smoke was a testament to the desperation of the villagers who, unable to wield arms or ignite fire themselves, had resorted to burning their own farms and huts in a symbolic act of protest and solidarity.

Terror gripped the whole village as households of prominent personalities in the village were burned up at night in their huts in a rage of vengeance. There was no going back until all had perished.

And indeed, all perished as the fire spread unchecked from one hut to another, from one farm to another. And finally, the fire spread into the pleasant land they had fought to possess. It burned up all the wood until the whole land was desolate.

Josi looked up into the smoke-filled air, with the fire still burning on the far side. He saw all gone. His sons were all gone, and so were his dreams that one day, the new fortune would give them all peace and prosperity. That night, his spirit departed with no one left to bury him.

CHAPTER THREE

For once, after several years in this forest, the brothers went out separately. Benju only wanted to go out into the forest to pick fruits, but Amah wanted to plough and plant seeds. Each of them went on with his plan for the day.

Amah had told his brother about the dream he had last night, which had continued into the new day, just as their father had dreamed. But Benju chose to believe in his own dream, not his father's or brother's. He feared that one day, this beautiful forest would become one big fire that could not be quenched. That was why he must gather as much as he could from the forest now.

The further Benju went into the forest, the more he saw its beauty. The cloud had given way to the bright sun, making the distant horizon clearly seen. The forest was bound on every side by hills and mountains. It was these hills and mountains that had to be climbed by whoever would find refuge in this forest. Many people wanted to come into the forest for refuge but could not ascend the mountains. That reduced the possible influx of people into the forest.

The hills had caves. Some popular old fables said the caves had hidden treasures. Inside these caves lived some hermits who had chosen this forest as their place of service. At first, there were twelve hermits living in twelve caves. Later, eight left the forest. Two became hunters, leaving only Lomu and Gideon as hermits in the forest.

A stream flowed from beneath the hills round the forest. Every dusk, the animals—the forest natives —descended down the hills to drink from its pure water. They would drink, filling their hearts with joy, and return uphill, leaving the plains to man and the small rodents.

The birds spread their wings to the fullest as they made their flights from the top of a tree to another, where they found something to nibble at. Flowers grew in every dense part of the forest, creating alluring sights before they shed their beauty at sunset.

I can do something to keep this forest from destruction. Benju thought. *I can live here forever. There's peace. There's everything I need to live long. Only if I can think of what to do to save this land, I must do something.* Slowly, Benju moved from the spot he had been and went deeper into the forest, his imagination to save the forest running wild with every step he took.

With only a small portion of his field remaining to be tilled, Amah quickly completed the task in a mere two hours. He had anticipated that his brother would have already returned from his journey to the forest by this time, and so he made his way back to their shared tent. However, upon arrival, he was met with an empty space, and his brother was nowhere to be seen, sparking a sense of concern and curiosity in Amah's mind.

He must have gone to the stream for his bath. Amah assured himself and waited for his return. After two hours of waiting in vain, Amah knew he had to go in search of Benju, his brother, along their usual path into the forest. He had to find him before sunset. Amah began trotting, sometimes off the narrow path. He was determined to find Benju wherever he had gone. He had gone out in search of him by lunchtime, which in the forest meant around 3:00 p.m.

Meanwhile, Benju's curiosity had led him inside a cave in one of the hills that bound the forest. He had noticed that particular hill before this time. But he was seeing the cave for the first time. Inside, it was very dark, but Benju was determined to get inside it, hoping to find some hidden treasures. He had heard interesting stories of the hidden treasures in the caves before. Several times, he hit himself against the rock in the cave and dashed his foot against stones. But he pressed on unconscious of the blood dripping coldly from his bruised feet, ankles and knees.

Benju continued to bleed in the cave. He could stand on his feet no more as his body began to hurt all over. He leaned against a rock in the cave and slowly lowered his body to sit down.

He thought to himself, *"If I call for help, no one will hear me."* He breathed with exertion, sprawling both arms and feet in the cave.

Now, Amah had followed every footmark he had noticed. He could not distinguish them as Benju's, but they could be his, and he hoped they were. The search took an hour, and Amah was tired since he had not had any meal the whole day. But he would not return without his brother.

The footprint Amah followed led him near the cave in which Benju sprawled helplessly. Amah stood at the mouth of the cave. Peeping into the cave, he found it very threatening. This was the last place on earth a person in his right mind would be. Benju could never be in that place. Amah reassured himself.

He stood up against the rock that bound the cave with both hands on the rock, looking into the bush around him. In that single moment, all the miseries he had had in life came back to his memory. He imagined that the worst was about to happen if he could not find his brother.

While Amah bowed his head in grief, two old men approached him unnoticed. They were monks who, once upon a time, had come into the forest but now had become hunters. They had approached Amah from behind a bend near the rock he leaned against.

"What are you after, young man?" One of them said. "Do not get in that cave. It is too dangerous."

"I am looking for my brother," Amah said, bowing. "I have searched everywhere in the forest, but still, I cannot find him."

"Can you describe your brother to us?" the other man asked. The two of them looked at each other, acting like they had found Benju.

"He is my brother," Amah explained. "He is only a little taller and bigger than me."

"Wait here for us," they both chorused as they departed from Amah, offering him some of the fruits in their hands when they noticed his exhaustion. "We shall help you find him."

Amah breathed a sigh of relief as he buried his teeth in the fruits given to him. Now, he had the hope of returning to the tent with Benju.

Returning from behind the same bend they had first approached Amah were the two old men with thirty strange young men. Amah ran to meet them, hoping to see Benju among them.

"Is your brother here?" one old man said.

"No, he's not," replied Amah. "Who are these?"

"They are those who have run into this forest for refuge," replied one of the old men. "We find more and more of them every day in the forest naked and without shelter."

Amah's heart sank in agony. The presence of these new faces in the forest meant that there were fresh wars beyond here.

"When will they go back to where they came from?" Amah asked sympathetically.

"No one knows," replied the old man. "We have to return to where we came from. We believe you'll find him."

Amah was disappointed. "But you can't go back!" He yelled. "You have to help me."

"How can we help you?" asked the old men in unison.

"We can go out in groups and look for my brother," Amah said. "I will lead one group."

"That is a good idea," said the first old man. "I will lead another group."

"I will lead another group, too," said the second old man eagerly.

"Young men!" The first old man bellowed as he raised his hands to give them orders. "Can you hear me well?"

"Yes!" they all yelled as he told them of their mission: to find Benju before sunset.

CHAPTER FOUR

Amah was leading the group in searching southeast of the rock. They had spread out in a line, with each man within hailing distance of the other. They had started off almost an hour ago but had still found nothing. Some of the young men decided it was time to go back under the trees where they had dwelt before as darkness sneaked up from behind them. But Amah and the two old men who were leading the other two groups kept convincing them that Benju was just around the next bend or under the next tree.

Just as the search party made their turns in different bends, Amah looked up and saw what he dreaded. Rain!

"Rain!" A member of Amah's group yelled. "What do we do now?"

"Proceed!" Amah replied, and they all proceeded.

"We have to return! Another shouted.

"It shall not rain." One old man assured. "It often does like this at this time of the year. Close to rain but no rain." They were all assured that it would not rain. But soon, the rain began in trickles and then in torrents.

The rain lashed their backs with fury, and the whiplash of lightning lit up the paths they were treading in an instant. Then, they were plunged back into the gloomy twilight, with the rumble of thunder urging them forward. The sun had dropped below the horizon unnoticed, and the night drifted down, gradually darkening the world around them.

They had stopped calling out Benju's name some time ago since their throats were sore and voices hoarse, and the rage of the storm swallowed their words before their ears could catch them. They shivered because of the cold.

Now, they needed to go under the tent, remove their wet clothes, and dry themselves near fires. But Amah kept convincing his group that Benju was just behind the next tree. The rain got worse until they could bear it no more. Everyone in the search party had to return to Amah's tent to continue the search after the rain.

Gideon had lived as a hermit in the caves on the hills bounding the eastern part of the forest. He had meditated and hunted in the nights for as long as anyone could remember. Only the grey-haired Lomu could possibly remember when he came into the forest, but unfortunately, Lomu was not good at remembering things beyond the stories and a few memories of wars that had taken place before he came into the forest. Lomu was also good at healing with herbs, while Gideon was good at setting snares.

Gideon was out very early one morning to check on the snares he had set the night before. On his way back, he passed by the rock that bound the cave Benju lay in. For the first time, he had an urge to beam his hunter's lamp into the cave. As he did, he peeped into the cave and sighted a glittering round mark on the rock. It was Benju's blood that glittered. Gideon saw the seemingly lifeless body lying beside the blood.

He got inside the cave, reached for Benju's body and carried him gently out of the cave with both arms. Outside the cave, he placed him down, bending over him to feel his pulse. He found him still breathing.

Gideon carried Benju to his cave close to Lomu's cave. Gideon's cave was a safe one wide enough for three to live in. Lomu had been here many times to tell Gideon stories.

While Benju lay unconscious in Gideon's cave, Gideon cleaned the blood on his body with a thick cloth dipped in hot water. At last, Benju began moving his body, still dreaming of the forest. In a moment, Benju opened his eyes and saw an unidentified bald head sitting beside him.

"Hello there! How was your sleep?" Gideon asked.

"Fine!" Benju mumbled, still confused with sleep, unable to take in the world around him.

"Here, have some broth, it'll warm you up." Gideon handed Benju a bowl of steaming soup with pieces of meat floating in it.

Benju accepted it and gulped it down greedily. The bowl was soon empty, and Gideon filled it again, smiling sagely. After that meal, Benju bathed and came out gasping at the cold shock.

Now Benju recollected all his last ordeals. Gideon asked him where he had come from. He replied that he had come from the largest clearing of the forest.

Later that day, they started off for Benju's tent. The search party organised for Benju was a great success. As they turned behind the trees and rocks, the search groups found human beings lying helpless on their backs. They were the latest entrants into the forest who had run and run until they got tired. Each of them was safely carried to the largest clearing where Amah lived, doubling the group's number within two days.

CHAPTER FIVE

The search groups continued searching the forest, not for Benju alone but for others who might be lying or wandering helplessly. When Gideon and Benju returned to the largest clearing in the intense heat of the afternoon, they were welcomed by the returned search groups with great joy.

Nothing in the history of the forest had called for jubilation like the return of Benju that afternoon. Later that day, Gideon and the two old men returned to their caves, leaving those they had rescued behind in the largest clearing. It was more comfortable living in the largest clearing than in the caves. Amah and Benju had spent years in the forest making the largest clearing and putting in place their tent with wooden poles and thatches. Now, they had a place to call home. Others chose to stay with them instead of returning to stay under trees.

As the weary refugees entered the largest clearing, their hearts, once heavy with fear of ferocious beasts, began to lift. The vast expanse of the clearing, coupled with the sight of smaller clearings nearby, kindled a spark of hope within them. The promise of safety and a fresh start began to overshadow their trepidation, replacing it with a sense of determination and renewed purpose. Benju's worries intensified. To him, this huge number of people meant disaster for the precious forest.

"How'll this place be preserved?" He thought. He felt for the forest. He felt for all in it, having dreamed of their imminent destruction.

Work began immediately in the largest clearing as Amah began to lead the refugees into the forest to cut down trees and build more tents. Everyone was eager to work except Benju, who was left to recover from his injuries. Thick drops of sweat fell from thin brows as the tents were being made. Benju sat down and wondered what might be done to save the forest from perils.

Early the following morning, Amah led the groups to his field of crops, where he had planted grains and some roots to support what the forest had. He led them through the grain fields that were near harvest. They saw the new pieces of land that was being ploughed. That took away all the fears they had had about surviving in the forest. Without any order, they bent their backs to plough. There was joy in them for the opportunity to start life all over again.

There were banana trees close to the largest clearing. In the past, the bunches had overripened and fallen off the trees. Amah and Benju occasionally ate from them whenever they were too tired to go into the forest for berries. Now, the refugees can't wait for them to be ripe again. The green bananas were plucked and roasted in a fire made near the tents to serve as daily meals. That continued for several days. Benju had warned all the other refugees to stay off the interior of the forest where the fruits grew in abundance.

That's the only way to save this forest. He reasoned. He supported himself by telling them the cause of his disappearance.

"When I went into the forest to pick fruits, I saw a pack of wolves and foxes feeding in the forest. They all ran after me. I ran and ran until I hid inside the cave where I got injured." That was the same story Benju had told Amah.

That story of the wolves and foxes in the forest filled all of them with terror. Without the protection of arms, the group opted for a cautious approach, settling in the largest clearing as a temporary haven. They relied on scavenging and foraging in the adjacent areas to sustain themselves, awaiting the day when the farm's crops would be ready for harvest, providing a more stable source of food and a chance to rebuild their lives.

Amah too stayed off the forest. But Benju went there unnoticed three times daily, returning with nothing each time he went. And so the tales of deadly wild beasts in the forest spread among the refugees, with Benju serving as a living witness to the horrors they could unleash on their unfortunate victims.

No one was forced to work on the farm. Amah, known for his strong work ethic, was surprised to find himself struggling to keep pace with the incredible productivity of his colleagues, Girusu and Khalisa. Despite his best efforts, he found it difficult to match their speed and efficiency as they worked together on the farm, leaving him to wonder at their seemingly boundless energy and dedication.

No one questioned Benju, who kept away from others both at work and at meals. He only joined at dusk to tell woeful tales of wolves in the forest and kept them off the forest. This earned him their regard as the master and protector of all the other refugees who starved himself for others to be filled and cared so much for their safety.

CHAPTER SIX

Around the largest clearing, there were shortages of food. All green bananas had been harvested and eaten, and there were two more weeks to the corn harvest. The few brave ones among the refugees considered going to the farthest ends of the forest to search for whatever they might find as food. But others persuaded them not to waste their lives for food, reminding them of the woeful tales of wolves.

For the next two weeks, they would have to live on the meagre food they could gather near the largest clearing. They reduced their meals to once a day. Sometimes, the older ones leave all the food to the younger ones. All this was expected to end in just two weeks.

While the other refugees were busy working on the farm, Benju would secretly venture into the forest, the very place where he had allegedly been attacked by wolves and foxes. At first, he went there three times daily. Later, he went there only once early in the morning, returning after sunset to avoid being noticed.

Benju's recent trips into the interior of the forest had given him many sorrows. He found many trees heavy with fruits, which, if not harvested, would be wasted. This was a special year in the forest. The trees produced more fruits than ever before as if they had expected to feed more people. Benju was baffled. He had not seen the trees with this much abundance of fruits. Before the fruits started getting ripe, falling off the trees, and rotting away, Benju knew he had to do something. He could not wait and see these precious fruits destroyed.

Real starving had begun in the largest clearing. Before the grains had a chance to mature, half of the grain field had already been devoured by desperate refugees who were unable to wait for the harvest. They plucked the unripe corns to find what to eat. A week before the corn was fully ripe, the field was almost consumed. But no one died among the refugees. That gave Amah joy. Though some were too sick to work. The sick ones might begin to die should food not be provided early enough.

"What shall we do to save these sick ones from dying?" Amah pondered and explained the situation to Benju, who had not noticed what was going on in the largest clearing.

"I think I'll risk my life and go into the forest to pick fruits for our people. I believe that the fruits are getting ripe by this time." Amah suggested.

"I can't let you go," Benju disagreed. "It's too dangerous in the forest. The wolves and foxes are there!"

"But we have to do something to help our people!" Amah said.

"Yes, we have to," agreed Benju. "I'll think of what to do. I'll solve the problem." Benju parted Amah on the back and left to sleep. That night, Amah filled all others with the hope that they would not die, assuring them that Benju would solve the problem of food shortage in the largest clearing.

Early the next morning, Benju had gone away from the largest clearing as he usually did. When he returned to the tent, he was with a large load of all sorts of fruits. This filled the other refugees with delight and hope of surviving again. The joy was seen all over their faces. They could not thank Benju enough for his benevolence. But before they sat down to enjoy the succulent products of the forest, Benju had something to tell them.

"Listen, everybody," Benju bellowed, prancing around them with calculated seriousness. He got all their attention and then proceeded to speak further.

"I have risked my life to get these for you. I did not want you to die. That's why I went into the forest where the beasts are to pluck these fruits."

"Thank you so much!" All echoed and bowed to him. He was delighted as he continued. "I promise to go there once in a day to pluck more for you."

"We'll go with you," Khalisa and Girusu, two of the refugees, offered.

"No, you can't." Benju responded, "Wolves are there!"

"We'll use sticks to fight them off!" Khalisa vowed.

"They'll outnumber you and kill you," said Benju. "They are very angry and hungry beasts." That sealed off everybody's lips.

Benju continued, "I'm the only one who can go into the forest because I know all about the foxes and wolves in this forest: where they stay, when they eat, when they wake and sleep, and the paths they follow."

"What if I follow you to help you carry the fruits down into the tents?" Amah suggested.

"No, you can't; it's too dangerous," replied Benju. "You're all I've got in this world. I don't want to lose you. Our voices might arouse the wolves from their sleep or hideout. That will arouse their anger, and they will attack us."

No suggestion was made to accompany Benju into the forest again, but they felt strong sympathy and gratitude for him having to risk his life for them. By the time the grains were ripe in the field, there was little left to harvest. Amah had advised that the remaining grains be left to dry to give them seed to plant. All obliged, having no more threat of starving to death as Benju was fulfilling his earlier promise to get them what to eat.

CHAPTER SEVEN

Long before planting, work had begun on the farm. The farm expanded day by day as every one of the refugees tasked himself with doing as much as Amah was doing. Benju made occasional visits to the farm. Every time he arrived, they all stopped working to salute him. He went through all the farms with short strides, inspecting all the work done with delight. On his last visit to the farm, Benju noticed a unique portion of the farm. There was more skill involved in that portion of the farm than the rest. The ridges were bigger, and the spaces between them were wider than the rest, with no weed growing between the rows.

Benju had thought that Amah must have worked on this unique portion of the farm until he enquired and realised he was wrong. That portion had been done by two people. They were Khalisa and Girusu. They had shown more skills than others on the farm. As of now, every man's work must be like theirs to be acceptable to Amah, and so others had to imitate them.

Khalisa and Girusu were not brothers; they were of the same lineage. Everyone could see that in the similar ancestral marks on their faces. Among their forefathers were farmers, hunters, and hermits. While growing up, they heard about their forefathers' heroic deeds. One planted a farm as large as a whole village. Another hunted a bear with sticks and stones. Yet, another left the comfort of their village to an unknown forest to live in as a hermit and has not returned to date.

All these stories filled their memories, and when war began in their village, they decided to show the hero in their family blood by making their flight into this unknown forest and escaping being sent to the battlefield as child soldiers. They had thought of hunting in the forest but for the gory tales of wolves in the forest that Benju kept telling them. They were the first to volunteer to follow Benju into the forest. That, too, had failed. Now, all they had to do to satisfy their desires was to work and work on the farm.

Benju admired Khalisa and Girusu for all he had found out about them. But he had one big fear about them. He feared that he might not succeed at keeping those two brave ones away from the forest for long. They might choose to go one day. That would endanger the forest. Benju was worried. He had seen in the characters of these two people that they could go into the forest. Amah had always seen Girusu and Khalisa as strength to others with the way they worked on the farm. But Benju began to see them as a real threat to his ambition to save the forest from destruction and be master in it.

Benju was wrapped up in gloom every time his mind wandered towards Girusu and Khalisa. He searched for ideas to ensure that they would not go into the forest. It was much easier for Benju to stop all the rest from going into the forest than to stop Khalisa and Girusu. But he got an idea.

Usually, Benju goes into the forest very early in the morning to bring fruits. The next morning, he went again but returned with nothing. He ran back to the largest clearing with great speed. It was evident that he was being chased. Khalisa was the first to see him coming.

"What's after you?" Khalisa said as he held him.

"W...w...wolves..." Benju said, panting as he pointed in the direction he had come from. Others who had come out of the tent ran back in. Girusu and Khalisa waited to see the wolves coming, but they saw nothing. Yet no one doubted that there were wolves after Benju.

"The wolves have spread all over the forest," Benju explained. "They now come out early in the morning."

Benju's story further heightened everyone's fear of wild beasts. But he knew that was not strong enough to deter Khalisa and Girusu from going into the forest, remembering Girusu's first suggestion.

"Can't we go out into the forest to attack the wolves?" Girusu had suggested.

"I think it's time we went," said Khalisa. "We must attack them before they attack us. Once they begin to smell our blood, they will never stop."

Benju was quick enough to discourage that, telling them how numerous the wolves were. "They're in thousands..."

Benju disappeared from the largest clearing again around afternoon, returning after sunset with a load of fruits and injuries on his body. Benju had intentionally injured his own feet with sharp stones in the forest, staging an illusion to deceive Khalisa and Girusu into believing that wolves were attacking people in the forest.

When Benju was asked what caused his condition again, he explained, breathing hard, "It's wolves. They nearly killed me. Three of them jumped on me!"

That scared them all. Not even Khalisa and Girusu ever thought of going into the forest again. Having succeeded in deterring Khalisa and Girusu from entering the forest, Benju set his heart on his next mission.

Now, I've saved the forest from destruction, he said to himself. *They'll never go there; the forest will be mine. It will be called Benju Forest. I'll be the master in this forest. I'll go around the forest, into the caves, and search for hidden treasures.*

Benju set his mind on the caves in the forest. Inside them, he hoped to find pearls of great worth, which he needed to establish himself as the master in the forest. Perhaps he might also find precious stones within the caves. He reassured himself that he would.

I need a lamp. He thought. *I can't go inside the caves without a lamp.* He pondered over how to get a lamp to take on his mission. That proved a setback. Then he remembered Gideon, who had rescued him the first time he went missing.

Gideon had a hunter's lamp he had kept since arriving in this forest. Benju remembered that lamp and loved to have it to take on his mission.

How do I get that lamp? Benju thought and smiled to himself, nodding in satisfaction like he already knew how.

CHAPTER EIGHT

Inside, Gideon's cave was dimly lit by a single oil lamp that cast a vague shadow on the side of the rock that bound the cave. Gideon had slept in the cave all night. Usually, Gideon slept a few hours after dinner, waking up by midnight to meditate till five in the morning when he would leave for the forest to check on the snares he had set the previous night, going with his hunter's lamp.

However, this night, Gideon had not woken up to meditate. He had slept all night without anything to remind him that it was midnight. He could not recollect when that ever happened to him before, nor could he explain the cause of it. He had not noticed what went on inside the cave while he slept. He could only recollect that an unknown tall figure had entered and passed out of his cave. But he had thought he was in a vision as he usually received visitations from unknown persons in his dream, giving him messages he needed to meditate over.

Discovering that it was nearly daybreak, Gideon startled up from the flat rock, the top of which was laid with banana leaves, that he had slept on. The oil lamp lit in the cave was still burning, and Gideon could see that it was nearly past the hour he went out to check his traps. He became gloomy for not having meditated for a whole night. He promised to make up for it by meditating all day instead of resting.

He must still go out to check on his snares, which seldom failed to make a catch. He turned to where he kept his hunter's lamp at the north end of the cave, but the lamp was not there.

He searched and searched inside the cave but could not find it. He remembered how he had kept it yesterday and had not touched it since then.

Gideon's mind pondered over what might have happened to his lamp. *Who might have taken it?* He thought. Only two people had ever been with him inside the cave, Lomu and Benju. He suspected none of them. Suddenly, his mind went back to the figure he had noticed while sleeping, walking slowly out of his cave. Then he had thought he was dreaming. Who could that be? He bowed his head in grief. He knew that his lamp was gone.

The lamp had been more than a hunter's lamp. It was a hermit's lamp as well. With it, Gideon had gone round the forest in the thick darkness of lonely nights meditating over the forest. He still lived with a dream he had on his first night in this forest. The dream was that one day, this forest would be inhabited by a huge number of people, too numerous to be counted. And peacefully too!

As more and more refugees began to escape into the forest, Gideon saw the fulfilment of his dream. He only hoped to see that dream come to pass. That was all he waited to see. Gideon mourned and mourned for his lamp into the new dawn. Of all he had brought into the forest, he had kept only the lamp. He had also come into the forest with a big pile of treasures—gold, diamonds, and other precious stones—which he had not kept with him in the cave. Both the lamp and the treasures were family heritage in his custody. His forefathers had passed them down for him to keep for the next generation.

Immediately Gideon arrived in the forest; he had kept the treasures in a large earthen pot and buried them somewhere in the forest. He could only identify where he had buried the treasures by the palm tree he had planted beside it. That was before he had found the cave he lived in. He had not checked them out ever since.

After breakfast, Lomu came to Gideon's cave. He had desired to talk with him all night, but he decided to wait until this morning when he was sure to find Gideon in the cave. The two had always shared their dreams of peace for the future. They had also shared everything, including meat and fruits. He entered the cave and found Gideon mourning, unaware of his presence.

"Hello there!" Lomu greeted. "Are you alright?"

There was no response. Gideon slowly lifted up his head and looked into Lomu's face with tear-filled eyes.

"The lamp's gone!" He whispered in tears.

"What lamp?" Echoed Lomu.

"My lamp!" Gideon replied. "The lamp of my fathers. It's gone..."

"Your lamp's not gone..." Lomu cut in sharply. "Your lamp can't go. No one can take your lamp from you. It's from heaven, not from your fathers." Gideon's face brightened up as he turned to listen more to the wisdom in Lomu's old voice.

"Your faith is your lamp." Lomu continued. "You believe that one day our children will live in peace and never die in wars; that's your lamp. It's burning in you. I can see it in your eyes. No one takes that from you." Lomu turned round and returned to his cave.

CHAPTER NINE

The first hurdle to Benju's mission had been scaled. He had secured a lamp. For the whole day, his face was beaming with joy. Every moment, his heartbeat raced up and down as he looked forward to catching the pearls of the forest. He knew this forest would have them amidst the rocks and in the dark caves. No one had probably conceived this idea of finding treasures in the forest. All anyone could think about were the fruits of the lush green trees. Benju could hardly wait to speak his parting words to Amah, who had gone with all the others to the farm.

In the night, when everyone had fallen into a deep sleep, Benju walked up to Amah, who was sleeping in the tent and roused him from his sleep. He began to talk to him with the lowest voice he could about his mission.

"I'm about to leave this place," Benju said. "I'll return soon. Don't look for me. And tell all others not to search for me. I'll come back to you."

"What about the wolves and foxes in the forest?" Amah said, looking into his eyes with anxiety.

"I'll escape from them as I have in the past," Benju assured. "Just warn everyone not to go into the forest. The wolves and foxes are there!"

Amah had not heard Benju speak of going out into the forest with this much boldness ever since he had first told them the tales of the wolves. He gave up trying to stop him from going into the forest and went back to sleep. Before the next dawn, Benju was out of the tent and out of the largest clearing.

It was not unusual to wake up and find Benju absent from the largest clearing. That happened so often, so no one inquired about his whereabouts when he had gone on his search for treasures. What was most dear to all the refugees living in the largest clearing were the words Amah told them every morning before going to the farm. That usually gave a beautiful start to every day.

This morning, Amah called all the other refugees to speak what would be his most memorable words:

"We're all very grateful to this forest for giving us a chance to live again. We're very grateful to the Creator of this forest. We're very grateful to every soul that ever lived in this forest for preserving it for us."

All nodded in gratitude. Amah continued. "We stand in the midst of a timeless thread, weaving together the past, present, and future. The forest's previous caretakers have passed on the tools and harvests, and we, in turn, will leave our own legacy for those yet to come, creating an unbroken chain of life and growth. That's exactly why we need to keep giving back to this forest that has given us so much. So let's start giving for the future..."

No one could doubt that this forest was once inhabited. As work continued on the farms, many farming tools were dug out of the earth, sharpened, and used. All the refugees had renewed determination to work harder than ever before, obviously encouraged by Amah's last words to them. They were all filled with the thought of giving something back to the forest. Amah added the order that the seeds of every fruit eaten must be planted. So gradually, all the fallow grounds of the forest were being tilled and sown.

One week turned into three, and Benju's absence sparked growing concern. Fears mounted that he had fallen prey to the forest's wolves. Khalisa proposed a search party, but Amah vetoed the idea, confident that Benju would return safely. However, as the days turned into weeks, Amah's assurances fell on deaf ears. The group began to lose hope, and soon, all but Amah were convinced that Benju had succumbed to the beasts.

Despite Amah's persistent assurances that Benju was still alive, the others started mourning him. Mourning for Benju took over the largest clearing, and farm work began to suffer. The refugees would suddenly drop their tools and begin wailing. Amah could not console them as they wept their hearts out for Benju, whom they believed had met his death while finding food for others.

For about two weeks, work stopped on the farm, and weeds began to take over gradually. The areas surrounding the largest clearing had once again been depleted of all the fruits that grew there since Benju had not returned with food as before.

The threat of starvation was inevitable should someone not take Benju's place and go into the forest for food. Amah dared not go since his brother had warned him not to. Fear of wolves kept everyone from going in search of Benju, whom they presumed dead. Starvation began in the largest clearing, more than the first they had experienced. No progress was noticed on the farm as they were too weak to work. When ever they went to farm, in less than an hour, they would retreated into their tents. Some of them could no longer step out of their tents as they became ill. The most terribly ill among the refugees was Benani, the youngest of all the refugees. Amah had often spared him the little he had to eat until there was nothing for anyone to eat.

All the refugees in the largest clearing, except the sick ones, kept vigil beside Benani, watching him like they were to stop his spirit from escaping out of the body which had grown so thin in the last few days. He could hardly move a step. Benani occasionally moved his head sideways but with pain. The last time he did, it was to look into the eyes of Amah, who knelt beside him as Benani muttered his last words to him:

"Thank you!" Then his eyes were closed, and all limbs stretched flat on the ground.

That silent night, the cruel hands of death seized Benani. It was the worst night ever experienced in the forest, but it later turned out to be the dawn of a new era for the dwellers of this forest. However, the weeping of the refugees for Benani's death continued for a long time.

CHAPTER TEN

The refugees decided to stop mourning and return to their farms to salvage the crops from weeds. Everyone but the sick ones returned to the farm twenty-one days after Benani was buried in a grave dug beneath the hill closest to the largest clearing. Not all who returned to the farm could work as before. Some were too hungry to work hard. Those who were strong enough among the refugees pressed on with the work on the farm, believing it was the only hope to stop more deaths in the largest clearing.

It suddenly became clearer to Khalisa that more death was inevitable in the largest clearing should an alternative source of food not be found. The sick ones may not last until the harvest in a month. Khalisa told Amah what his plan was.

"We can't just stand by and watch people die of hunger. We need to do something."

"I'm worried too," said Amah. "What can we do?"

"We can go into the forest just as Benju did and search for fruits," Khalisa said.

"Is that not too dangerous?" Amah asked.

"What's more dangerous is for all these sick ones to die of hunger," Khalisa responded.

"Yes, you're right," agreed Amah. "We can do something."

Amah told Girusu of their plan to go into the forest, which Benju had told them was a danger zone, and get fruits into the largest clearing.

"I think that's the right thing to do," said Girusu. "I'll go with you."

"No, you can't go with us," Amah responded. "You stay behind, and let's be sure of the dangers involved. If we fail to return on time, know that we are in danger and organise a search for us."

Early the next morning, around the time Benju usually left for the forest, Amah and Khalisa ventured into the interior of the forest, which Benju had forbidden them to go into for so long.

They went with sharp tools in their hands to fight wild beasts that might attack them. They were determined in their hearts to fight any wolf that intruded on their mission. They made up their minds not to give up on their mission no matter the danger until they had gone back to the largest clearing with succulent fruits to revive those dying souls there.

"We must not go back empty-handed," Khalisa said with strong determination in his voice. "No one will starve to death again."

As they went along cautiously, they looked under the bush for a wolf or fox possibly lurking there. They spoke in hushed voices lest they arouse the wolves and foxes from their hideouts.

At last, they were at the forbidden spots, from where they would not go any further because, as they looked up and down, they saw fruits in abundance. The trees were laden with ripe fruits, and the ground was covered with all sorts of rotten fruits. No wild beast was in view.

With urgency and caution, Amah plucked the ripe fruits from the trees while Khalisa stood guard, scanning the surroundings for any sign of wolves. Time was of the essence, as they knew that lingering too long would increase their risk of encountering the wolves. Once they had collected a sufficient amount of fruits to nourish the sick refugees in the largest clearing, they promptly and carefully made their way back, retracing their steps to ensure a safe return. Back in the largest clearing, the sick were the first to be fed. After they had eaten, there was nothing left for others to eat. So Amah and Khalisa had to repeat their trip to the forest. Again, they returned with fruits, this time enough to satisfy everyone in the largest clearing.

For the next three days, Amah and Khalisa went into the forest to find food for the rest of the refugees without any threat to their lives from wolves.

"Did you see the wolves or foxes?" Girusu asked them after they had just returned from the forest one morning.

"No, we didn't," replied Amah. "It's like wolves don't come out in the morning."

From now on, the story began to circulate among the refugees that wolves don't come out in the morning but at night. This increased their desire to go into the forest and see the trees that bore the fruits that had sustained them.

The first person to go with Amah and Khalisa was Girusu. He came back with the same story that there were no wolves in the forest. Now, everyone had the boldness to go into the forest in the morning and find what to eat before starting work on the farm. When they reached the forest, they were filled with bitter hatred for Benju as they saw what he had denied them for too long.

They hated Benju the more as they thought of Benani. Had there been enough to eat, Benani would not have died, they reasoned. The hatred for Benju now filled the largest clearing as they found more and more reasons to doubt all the tales he had told about wolves in the forest.

Amah could not explain why Benju would tell such terrible lies to keep others in misery. "Perhaps he saw the wolves at night," he thought.

When Amah told Khalisa that Benju might have seen the wolves at night, they decided to test that by going to the forest at night. They took cover in the thickets all night, watching for wolves. They returned to the largest clearing the next dawn, having sighted no wolf all night.

CHAPTER ELEVEN

Gradually, the tale of deadly wild beasts that had long bound the refugees to the largest clearing disappeared from their minds. Those tales were now seen as a product of Benju's cruel imagination to make them suffer. Now, they saw everywhere in the plains of the forest as a safe place to live, and they began to see the largest clearing as too small a place for them all to live.

"This place is too small for us to live," Khalisa said. "We have to clear more land and build more tents in the forest."

No one objected to Khalisa's words, and the next morning, they began extending their tents into the interior of the forest that they had once dreaded.

All the refugees in the largest clearing were to be divided into three groups to do the work. There was also the last weeding to be done on the farm before harvest. A group of about twenty led by Girusu was in charge of that. Another group of almost the same size, led by Khalisa, was in the dense part of the forest, cutting down trees and thatches to make the tents. Amah led the rest to make the tents in the very places Benju had warned them to stay clear of.

One afternoon, while they were making the tents in the forest's plains, two unexpected visitors came to them. They were Gideon and Lomu. They had seen from their caves that the forest was covered by people, just as they had seen in their dreams. It was a sign of the peace they believed would start from this forest and spread beyond it.

Gideon and Lomu had been out this morning in search of the treasures Gideon had kept in an earthen pot and buried in the ground when he had first come into the forest. Gideon wanted to recover them and keep them in Lomu's cave since there was once a mysterious theft in his own cave. Gideon was so anxious to recover the treasures. He feared that those treasures could throw the forest into chaos should any of the refugees find them. A tussle for the treasures might ensue among the refugees, leading to big trouble. This thought had given Gideon sleepless nights since he had seen the refugees building the tents around where he had hidden the treasures.

Gideon's search for the treasures was in vain because he could not remember the exact spot where he had buried them. The entire forest was no longer the same, and none of the trees around where Gideon had buried the treasures were still standing.

"The treasures shall be found," Lomu said, and Gideon was consoled, having learned to trust Lomu's words.

Gideon's visit to the refugees, where they made the new tents, turned out to be an occasion of reunion with his great-grandchildren. Khalisa was just returning with a load of thatches on his head when he saw Gideon. He could identify Gideon as his great-grandfather – the eccentric hermit, about whom many stories had been told. What struck him was the uncanny resemblance, particularly their identical facial markings! Khalisa dropped the load on his head and fell into Gideon's warm embrace. Khalisa called Girusu, who was working on the farm, to see their great-grandfather. Later, both of them followed Gideon to his cave, where they remained with him till sunset before returning to the largest clearing.

Gideon's joy knew no bounds for seeing two of his descendants again. He had lived with the fear that all his descendants might have been wiped out by war in their native land. On their last visit to his cave, he poured out his heart to them, reflecting on his life so far in the forest and the dreams he had for the future.

"This forest has been a wonderful home for all of us," Gideon said. "A good place to live in peace." He kept quiet for a while. "I thank God that I came into this forest. I have fulfilled my days on earth in service to the future generation."

"Father," Girusu said. "Did you meet some people in this forest?"

"Yes, I did," Gideon responded. "Many people, including my old mentor, Lomu and some other people."

"What happened to those people?" Khalisa asked.

"They all left the forest," Gideon responded. "For two years, there was no rain in the forest, making life unbearable for all of us. Some died, some left, but we chose to stay."

"Were you and father Lomu the only hermits that came into the forest?" Khalisa asked.

"No, my son," Gideon responded. "We were twelve living in twelve caves. Eight of us left during the drought, and two became hunters."

"What's the worst thing that ever happened to you in this forest, father?" Girusu asked. Gideon paused for a moment and looked into the eyes of both men in his cave.

"The lamp!" He burst out. "The lamp was taken away in this cave. I inherited the lamp from my father. It would have been my great joy to give the lamp to you, but it's... it's... taken...away..."

"Was that all you brought into this forest, father?" Khalisa asked.

"I also brought a pile of precious treasures meant to be kept for my descendants. They are our family heritage. But now I can't find them."

Gideon's voice was thick with regrets as he fought back tears, making Khalisa and Girusu stop asking more questions and leave for their tents.

CHAPTER TWELVE

All tents but one had been made. Amah had to dig deep to erect the pillar of the last tent. Each tent had four pillars in its four corners. As Amah was digging the ground for the last pillar of the last tent, he found a wonder. The tool he dug with made a strange, coarse sound as it made contact with the earth. Amah dug further until he saw an earthen pot with treasures in it. The pot was broken, but the treasures were intact. He carefully removed every piece of the treasures, packing them to his tent in the largest clearing and stopped work for that day.

When Amah showed the treasures he had found to Khalisa, he suggested that they be kept with Gideon in his cave. Later that evening, they departed for Gideon's cave, hurrying to get there before darkness.

Gideon was surprised to see them at this late hour of the day, as he was just about to get inside his cave. Darkness was about to spread all over the forest, and Gideon had begun to perceive strange evil lurking in darkness somewhere within this forest.

"Why have you come?" Gideon asked. "This forest is no longer safe in darkness."

"We've brought this to you, father," Amah said as he gave the pile of treasure to Gideon.

"Return now!" Gideon commanded without assessing what he had just collected. "Don't walk in the night without a lamp."

They perceived danger in Gideon's warning and began to run back to the largest clearing to avoid darkness catching up with them. Gideon observed them from a distance, watching as they hurriedly retreated to their tent, his gaze following them until they disappeared from his sight.

"If I still had my lamp, I would have followed them with it." Gideon shook his head as he entered his cave.

The thought of Gideon's lamp had never left him. Every night, he thought about it. As he opened the pile he carried, tears rolled down his cheeks. He remembered Lomu's words that had said,

"You shall find the treasures."

"I believe I will find the lamp as well," Gideon said, smiling.

CHAPTER THIRTEEN

The lamp had been out the previous night while Benju was searching for treasures in one of the caves. Benju had not gone with additional oil for the lamp, so when the oil was finished, the lamp went out. That night, Benju tried to get out of the cave in the dark, but it proved too hard. He decided to sleep inside the cave until daybreak when reflections of the daylight would help him get out.

Though Benju had been out in search of treasures for about four months, he had not found a single one. Day after day, he refreshed himself with the fruits of the trees and continued his search. Inside the caves, he only found old farming tools, which he did not take.

Benju opted to withdraw from the treasure hunt and make his way back to the safety of the largest clearing, leaving the remaining rocks, hills, and caves unexplored for the time being. He prioritised caution over the allure of potential riches. So, just before sunset, Benju set off for the largest clearing, ready to tell more woeful tales of wolves.

"They'll run to meet me," Benju thought. "I'll give them plenty of fruits to eat and tell them more stories. They'll be happy again."

Benju was walking as fast as he could to reach the plains of the forest, where he was sure to find the trees heavily loaded with ripe fruits without anyone to eat them.

My trees must have been waiting for me to harvest their fruits. Benju thought. In a moment, he stood still in a strange manner, like a still voice had commanded him to move no more. He could not identify the world around him again. He looked blindly around him to find a clue to help him understand where he stood. He saw new tents where there were nothing but bushes before.

"Where am I?" He questioned as he looked round again and saw the fallen trees. "They have come here. They have destroyed this forest. Amah had done this. He'll pay for it. I will make him pay. He had brought those people into this place." He burst into tears, "I have been away for too long. I have not come back with anything. Now the forest has been taken from me. I'll kill Amah for this. I'll pull down these tents.

Benju struck the tents with heavy sticks to break them, but the pillars stuck firmly to the ground, refusing to fall. In the end, he gave up trying to pull down the tents.

"Alright," he said, panting. "I'll leave the tents, but I'm going to kill Amah... and Khalisa...And Girusu... they have done this..." Benju marched on to the largest clearing in a fury. "They must not see me. They'll kill me. I need to hide in the bush." He took cover around the largest clearing, armed with heavy sticks, waiting for his would-be victims to come out of the tent and meet their end one after another as darkness gradually spread its curtain over the largest clearing.

Khalisa and Amah were running back to the largest clearing from Gideon's cave. They were running as fast as they could, breathing fast. When they reached the new tents on their way to the largest clearing, they had to stop.

"See this," Khalisa said, pointing to the lamp Benju had left behind. It's a lamp."

"I know," Amah responded, "take it and let's go. Hurry up!"

Khalisa took the lamp. "It's for my father," he said, facing the opposite direction. I must return it to him."

"What!" Amah exclaimed, confused, as Khalisa ran back in the opposite direction. Amah ran after him and yelled, "father said it's dangerous to walk in the dark." Khalisa had gone too far to hear him.

Amah turned back towards the largest clearing, where others were awaiting their arrival. As Amah ran round the last bend to the largest clearing, Benju suddenly rushed across his path, tripping him. Benju struck him with his stick once and again until he was sure that he was dead. Benju's fury was not yet spent as he disappeared into the darkness of the forest.

CHAPTER FOURTEEN

Gideon was elated. "Thank you, my son," he said happily.

"You have brought back to me all that I have lost. "His face lit up in ecstasy as he collected the lamp Khalisa had brought back to him, refilled it with oil and lit it again.

"I have to go back father," said Khalisa. "Amah is waiting for me."

"I'll follow you to your tent with my lamp." Gideon offered. "I perceive that evil is lurking in the dark somewhere in this forest."

"No, father, I can go by myself." Khalisa insisted.

"No, you can't," Gideon disagreed. "I'll go with you."

They started going to the largest clearing in the darkness of the night since the moon had refused to shine.

Khalisa had expected Amah and others to be awake awaiting his arrival, as it was their custom to see everyone safely in the tent before going to sleep. Gideon and Khalisa stood abruptly as they saw a body lying in the bush, in his own blood. It was Amah where he had been struck down by his brother.

"It's Amah!" Khalisa yelled as he fell on the body drenched in blood. Gideon moved Khalisa aside and bent low to carry Amah to his tent, where he would be attended to as Khalisa followed with the lamp.

As Amah's life hung in the balance, Gideon knew every moment counted. The severity of Amah's blood loss demanded immediate attention, and Gideon was all too aware of the urgency. He quickly took Amah into his cave and rushed to fetch Lomu, who is skilled and renowned for his expertise in treating severe injuries with natural remedies. However, even Lomu's vast experience had never been tested by a wound as critical as Amah's. The gravity of the situation weighed heavily on Gideon's mind, filling him with doubt about Amah's chances of survival.

As Lomu entered Gideon's cave and saw Amah in his wounds, he said, "he'll live." Those words filled Khalisa with great joy. Immediately, Lomu began squeezing different herbs and fruits into Amah's mouth and wounds. They had to remain in Gideon's cave while Amah's treatment lasted. It took days for Amah to be fully conscious of his environment. The first person he noticed around him was Khalisa, who was watching over him while Gideon was out for food and Lomu for herbs.

Slowly, with wonder, Amah recalled his last ordeal and his attacker but chose not to speak. Lomu had warned that Amah must not leave the cave since he still had difficulty moving certain parts of his body. He obliged, filled with gratitude to Lomu and Gideon for saving his life.

Gideon had gone to the largest clearing to inform the refugees there that Amah and Khalisa would not return until Amah had fully recovered from the wounds he had. Learning that Amah had been wounded reminded all the refugees in the largest clearing of the tales of wolves Benju told them. Perhaps those tales were true. Perhaps Amah had been wounded by wolves, they all thought. The fear of wild beasts gripped them once more. It then became evident to them all that there was real danger in the forest. They resumed their caution, keeping to the largest clearing as before.

"I have perceived long ago that danger lurks in the dark in this forest," Gideon said to Lomu while they discussed whatever might have attacked Amah. "But I don't know what that evil might be."

"The evil will soon be found out," Lomu said. "It'll be found out and stopped. No evil will survive in this forest. Peace will reign."

Meanwhile, Benju's fury was more than ever before. He said in bitter tears, "I have lost everything. I have lost the forest. I have lost the lamp as well. They'll all pay for this."

The day finally came when Gideon had promised to bring Amah back to the largest clearing. Accompanied by Lomu, they set off for the largest clearing after sunset. Their journey to the largest clearing had been deliberately delayed till after sunset because Lomu had said that night that the evil in the forest would be found out and stopped. Girusu was the most anxious of all the refugees in the largest clearing awaiting Amah's return. He had stood in front of his tent, peering in the direction of Gideon's cave, expecting them to make the two-and-half-hour journey back.

Either Khalisa or Girusu was Benju's next target. He had taken cover in the bush near the largest clearing, expecting either of them to pass. Unfortunately, Girusu became the next victim as he walked near Benju's lurking place. He was struck thrice with a stick in different parts of the body. But he was strong enough to shout, forcing others to run out of their tents. They saw Girusu down and Benju fleeing. Some went for Girusu, some for Benju. Before long, both were in their hands.

Raucous rumble took over the largest clearing as they gripped Benju in their hands, dragging him to a tree to be tied while he struggled to free himself from the tight grips.

"Benju's the only wolf in this forest!" one of them said, fuelling their hatred for him even more. He was securely tied to a tree and watched by about a dozen of them. Others struggled hard to revive Girusu.

Usually, the journey from Gideon's cave to the largest clearing takes less than three hours. But Amah's return to the largest clearing in Lomu's company ended up taking about four hours because Amah could not move as fast as before, reducing others' pace as well.

Benju's fate had been left till Amah's arrival. But the rumble in the largest clearing had not subsided yet. It was in the midst of the chaos that had erupted among the refugees in the largest clearing that Amah and those who accompanied him appeared. It had taken quite a while for them to be noticed as the refugees were occupied in the confusion that had overtaken the largest clearing, all yelling at Benju for the disaster he had unleashed on them. They would have sought vengeance but only for Amah, whom they all loved so dearly.

Amah looked over at the mob, seeing Girusu lying helplessly on the ground and Benju tied securely to a tree. Amah shook his head in disappointment. He had seen them long before anyone in his company did. They eventually halted at the largest clearing, watching from behind one of the tents and hearing all the insults the refugees were hurling at Benju. Amah just wept and wept.

Lomu stepped into the midst of the mob, with all others with him. For the first time since arriving at the largest clearing that night, their presence was noticed, and all the yelling subsided. There was calmness as each of the refugees took his turn to welcome them, bowing before Lomu and Gideon.

Lomu saw Benju tied to the tree where he could not even raise up his head. Gideon, too, saw him and recognised him as the one he had rescued in the cave before. But their first priority was to heal Girusu. They had to carry Girusu to Gideon's cave to be properly treated. Khalisa and another refugee volunteered to carry him to the cave. As they were about to depart, Gideon beamed his lamp into Benju's face like he wanted to be sure of his identity. That drew all attention to him.

"That's the only danger in this forest," Lomu said. "He's the evil that lurks in the night in the forest. Let him remain tied till we are back." They carried Girusu to the cave for proper treatment.

CHAPTER FIFTEEN

Three days and three nights had gone since Benju was tied to a tree. He had not been given food or water. He had spent these three last days and nights reclining against the tree he was tied to, often lost in his thoughts.

"Now, I'm in pain." He lamented. "I'm hungry. Now I know what it is to be in pain. I have caused so much pain and misery for others. I don't deserve to live. I'll kill myself."

The thought of killing himself had filled Benju since he was tied to the tree.

"I can't live among these people again." He thought in silence. "They'll never forgive me for all that I have done to them."

In the desolate silence, Benju's isolation deepened, with no one coming to his aid or even to check on him. As the hours dragged on, his hopelessness grew, and he began to ponder the darkest of options – ending his own life. The desperation that had been building inside him now seemed to have only one possible outlet, and Benju's thoughts became increasingly consumed by the means to escape his unbearable situation through death. Amah expected Lomu to return soon, pardon Benju, and set him free. But now Lomu's return had taken longer than expected. How long could Amah bear seeing his brother in pain? Amah went to Benju secretly in the dead of the night and aroused him from his thoughts.

"Hello there," Amah said, "take this and eat." He offered him some fruits.

"No, I don't want," said Benju. "I want to die. I don't deserve to live."

"No, you won't die," assured Amah. "We all deserve to live."

"I'm very sorry, Amah," said Benju, "I'm sorry for what I did to you and others. I went out of my mind."

"I've long forgiven you," Amah said. "Just say sorry to all others, and they'll forgive you as well."

"They will?" Benju asked, amazed.

"Yes, they will," Amah replied.

After breakfast the next morning, Girusu was returning to the largest clearing fully recovered. He was accompanied by Lomu, Gideon, Khalisa, and the other refugees who had carried him to Gideon's cave. As they got to the tents, all the refugees came out to meet them, eagerly waiting for Lomu's verdict on Benju.

Having seen their expectations from their eyes, Lomu spoke.

"There he is, your friend, your brother. You need to forgive him." There was no immediate response from anyone as Lomu began to untie Benju from the tree. When he was free, he stood in the centre of the circle formed by the gathering.

"What does it cost to say sorry?" Gideon said as he touched Benju on the shoulder. "Just say sorry to them all."

Slowly, Benju went on his knees, and tears rolled down his cheeks. Everyone had compassion for him as he wept. Then Amah came into the centre of the circle, speaking with tears:

"This is our brother, not our enemy. Though he did us much evil, he has taught us all we need to learn to survive in life. He has taught us how to survive against hunger even in the midst of plenty. He has taught us how to conquer our fear of the forces of nature and wild beasts, which are products of our imaginations. And above all, through what he did, we have learnt that we can stop war even with all our differences. Now, I know that if we can tolerate what my brother did to us, we can tolerate whatever we do against one another, and we can live together in peace."

Everyone nodded in approval as Amah finished speaking. Their long hatred for Benju disappeared instantly. Lomu and Gideon saw the need to return to their caves, seeing their aim of uniting all the refugees at the largest clearing accomplished.

"Father, please don't leave me," Benju shouted as they turned to go. Their movement was interrupted by Benju's plea. Benju fastened his eyes on Gideon, pleading.

"Don't leave me here, father. Please, I want to go with you. I want to learn to be good and care for others."

Gideon gestured to Benju to come along with him, and he followed him, bidding the largest clearing a tearful farewell.

www.ingramcontent.com/pod-product-compliance
Lightning Source LLC
LaVergne TN
LVHW041253150826
845673LV00008B/2578